IGOR'S LAB OF FEAR

A JAR OF EYEBALLS

by Michael Dahl   illustrated by Igor Šinkovec

STONE ARCH BOOKS
a capstone imprint

Igor's Lab of Fear is published by Stone Arch Books
A Capstone Imprint
1710 Roe Crest Drive, North Mankato, Minnesota 56003
www.capstonepub.com

Cataloging-in-Publication Data is available at the Library of Congress
website.
Hardcover ISBN: 978-1-4965-0455-5
Paperback ISBN: 978-1-4965-0459-3
Ebook ISBN: 978-1-4965-2320-4

SUMMARY: Kevin is tired of being ignored. No one in school ever seems
to notice him, so he decides to win the school science fair prize — no
matter what it takes. But Kevin soon finds himself up to his eyeballs
in trouble.

DESIGNER: Kristi Carlson

Printed in China by Nordica
0716/CA21600955
052016   009799R

TABLE OF CONTENTS

Ah, it's you again!
Come in! Come in!

Was the door hard
to open?

It probably needs
more **SLIME** on
the hinges.

Just give it a shove.

Don't worry. You'll be able to get back out. Hehe.

So nice of you to stop by.

I always enjoy visitors to my lab.

Ahh, I see you're admiring my jar of eyeballs.

Are they *real*, you ask?

Well, that's an interesting story . . .

CHAPTER ONE
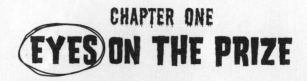# EYES ON THE PRIZE

Kevin had sharp eyes.

No one at school ever noticed Kevin.

But he noticed <u>everyone</u> and everything.

Kevin's eyes liked bright, shiny objects.

They especially liked the trophy in
the glass case outside the school office.

Kevin was determined to win that prize.

Then people would <u>notice</u> him.

Then he would be famous.

All eyes would be on him.

CHAPTER TWO
EYEBALLS

Kevin knew nothing about science.

But he knew about science fairs.

At every fair he visited, there was always one exhibit that was the same.

A jar of cow eyes sitting on a table.

And a poster explaining how eyes worked.

I could do that, thought Kevin. *I don't even have to study.*

Kevin had a plan to make sure he'd win.

His exhibit would have so many eyes in it. More than any other exhibit in the world. There was no question about that.

The real question was: Where would he find the eyes?

CHAPTER THREE
FILLING THE JARS

For weeks, Kevin worked alone in his basement every night.

His collection of jars grew bigger and bigger.

Each jar was filled with eyeballs.

They rolled and bobbed up and down in **SNOT-GREEN** liquid.

Perfect, Kevin thought.

It was just the beginning.

He marked the days on a calendar hanging on the wall.

Soon, the science fair was only a *week* away.

I need MORE eyes! he realized.

CHAPTER FOUR
AT THE FAIR

At last, the night of the science fair arrived.

Hundreds of people came to the fair.

They walked through the aisles
and looked at the exhibits.

Everyone stopped to look at
Kevin's countless jars.

His exhibit had the most visitors.

"Where did you get so many eyes?" asked one of the judges.

Kevin grinned.

"Oh, all sorts of places," he said.

Some of Kevin's visitors felt dizzy or strange when they looked at the eyes.

"That looks just like my mom's eye," said a young girl, pointing.

"This eye reminds me of our substitute teacher," said an older boy. "The one we had last week."

A tall man pointed to the biggest jar in Kevin's exhibit.

The jar held a floating eye as large as a soccer ball.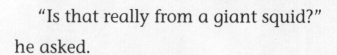

"Is that really from a giant squid?" he asked.

Kevin nodded. "My uncle is a scientist," he said. "He studies underwater animals. He got it for me."

All three judges took careful notes.

When they left, Kevin's own eyes gleamed.

He could almost <u>feel</u> the shiny trophy in his hands . . .

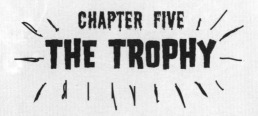

CHAPTER FIVE
THE TROPHY

At the end of the night, the judges made their decision.

No one was surprised when Kevin won first prize.

He held the trophy up high so everyone would see that he was the <u>winner</u>.

I tricked them! he said to himself. *Now they see me.*

When Kevin got home, he put the trophy in his room.

He stood and admired it.

He rubbed his hands together and laughed. Ha ha ha ha ha Ha ha ha ha ha!

"If they only knew," Kevin said. "Those weren't even real eyeballs."

CHAPTER SIX
ALL EYES ON HIM

Kevin dreamed about eyes that night.

He dreamed about all his hard work in the basement.

He had made the eyes from
dozens of stolen balls.

Ping-pong balls. Billiard balls.
Racquetballs.

The giant
squid eye was
really a kickball

he'd stolen from the school's gym.

In his dream, all the eyes in the
jars began to **mOVe**.

They all turned and stared at him.

Then Kevin woke up from his
nightmare. He was breathing hard.

"It was only a dream," Kevin said.

He started rubbing his eyes, then
he stopped. He stared at his hands.

An eyeball was growing in
his palm.

He pulled up his sleeve. Dozens of
eyeballs peered out of his skin.

He was **COVERED** in eyeballs!

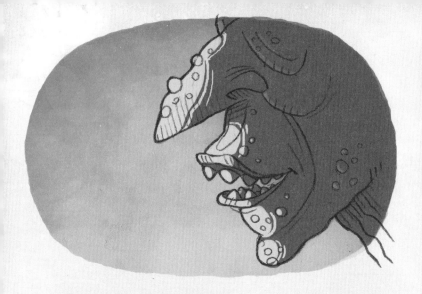

Do you *see*, reader? Kevin wanted
to be famous. He wanted attention.

He wanted all eyes on him.

Well, he got what he wished for,
<u>didn't he?</u>

Oh, must you go so soon?

Take a fake eyeball as a souvenir.

At least . . . I *think* it's fake!

PROFESSOR IGOR'S LAB NOTES

Eyes are weird. Weirder than me, even. But don't take my word for it — *see* for yourself. Hehe.

Ever notice those strange squiggly things in your vision that look like little bugs? Those are actually shadows of small protein strands inside your eyes, not crazy critters. We do have microscopic creatures lurking in our eyelashes, though.

Just be thankful you aren't a bee. They have hairy eyeballs! The hairs play an important role in helping them detect their speed and the direction of the wind while they fly.

Some species of animals like dolphins and ducks sleep with one eye open. That way they can stay safe from nocturnal predators. Also, it freaks out their parents.

There is a pair of conjoined twin girls in Canada who are connected at the brain. They can see through each other's eyes. If you ever feel like living with your siblings stinks, imagine sharing your eyes with them!

GLOSSARY

ADMIRING (ad-MY-er-ing)—feeling respect or approval for someone or something

DETERMINED (di-TER-muhnd)—if you are determined to do something, then you are going to do it no matter what

ESPECIALLY (ih-SPESH-uh-lee)—very much or more than usually

EXHIBIT (ig-ZIB-it)—an object or a collection of objects that have been put out in a public space for people to look at

GLEAMED (GLEEMD)—shined brightly

HINGE (HINJ)—a usually metal piece that attaches a door, gate, or cover to something that allows it to open and close

INTERESTING (IN-ter-rest-ing)—if something is interesting, it attracts your attention and makes you want to learn more about it

SOUVENIR (soo-ven-EER)—something that is kept as a reminder of someone, somewhere, or something

DISCUSSION QUESTIONS

1. Was Kevin's jar full of real eyeballs? Explain your answer.

2. Why do you think Kevin wanted to win the Science Fair? Did he want the prize, or something else?

3. Does this story have a moral? What do you think the point of this story is?

WRITING PROMPTS

1. Do you think Igor is telling the truth about Kevin's story? Write down three reasons that support your answer.

2. Write another chapter to this story. What does Kevin do after he sees all the eyeballs on his arms? What happens to him?

3. Make up a biography for Professor Igor. Who is he? What does he do for a living? Why does he chuckle so much? You decide.

AUTHOR BIOGRAPHY

Michael Dahl, the author of the Library of Doom, Dragonblood, and Troll Hunters series, has a long list of things he's afraid of: dark rooms, small rooms, damp rooms (all of which describe his writing area), storms, rabid squirrels, wet paper, raisins, flying in planes (especially taking off, cruising, and landing), and creepy dolls. He hopes that by writing about fear that he will eventually be able to overcome his own. So far it isn't working. But he is afraid to stop, so he continues to write. He lives in a haunted house in Minneapolis, Minnesota.

ILLUSTRATOR BIOGRAPHY

Igor Sinkovec was born in Slovenia in 1978. As a kid he dreamt of becoming a truck driver — or failing that, an astronaut. As it turns out, he got stuck behind a drawing board, so sometimes he draws semi trucks and space shuttles. Igor makes his living as an illustrator. Most of his work involves illustrating books for kids. He lives in Ljubljana, Slovenia.